Fern Hollow is a wonderful place to live. Ask Professor Sigmund Swamp or old Brock Gruffy to tell you about their lovely little village, and they will talk all day and yet hardly have begun.

They will tell you that Fern Hollow nestles at the foot of the trees of Windy Wood and that through the village runs the sparkling ribbon of the River Ferny.

The animals of Fern Hollow are all good friends and neighbours, and if you are a stranger, they will make you feel at home in next to no time.

BROCK THE BALLOONIST

Written & Illustrated by John Patience

Published by Haddock Ltd., Bridlington, England
© Fern Hollow Productions Ltd.
Printed in Italy
ISBN 0 7105 0283 4

Brock Gruffy bustled around his little shop, puffing on his pipe like an old steam engine. He was trying to tidy the place up, but it was in such a terrible clutter that it was an almost impossible task. Brock was soon distracted from the job when he came across an enormous cardboard box which he couldn't remember having seen before.

"What's this?" he muttered, adjusting his spectacles to read the label.

"HOT AIR BALLOON"

"How exciting!"

Brock dragged the box (which was very heavy)
out into his garden, and, following the
instructions, soon had the balloon inflated.
It was striped red and yellow and was
absolutely gigantic!

The badger climbed into the basket and untied the anchor rope, and the balloon floated up into the clear blue morning sky. Higher and higher it climbed until the houses of Fern Hollow looked like tiny little models. Soon Brock began to feel dizzy and decided to bring the balloon down a little. Unfortunately the silly badger let out far too much air and found himself speeding towards the church steeple.

"Oh no!" cried Brock, covering his eyes.

CRUNCH
the basket hit the steeple
and sent it crumbling
to the ground!

Parson Dimly came rushing out of
the vicarage, thinking that there
must have been an earthquake,
and was amazed to see the enormous
balloon floating away across the
River Ferny, with Brock Gruffy
in the basket waving his arms around
and shouting for help.

At last the balloon came down on top of Sigmund Swamp's roof, crashing into his bedroom and giving the poor Toad, who was still in bed, the fright of his life.

Soon a crowd of animals had gathered around Sigmund's house, and P.C. Hoppit arrived on his bicycle looking very serious. Of course Brock couldn't afford to pay for all the damage he had done, and P.C. Hoppit had no alternative but to arrest him.

What a terrible thing to happen! Brock Gruffy was locked up in Fern Hollow jail and feeling, as you might imagine, very sorry for himself.

THE BRASS BAND ROBBERY

One morning a large wooden crate arrived on the goods
train at Fern Hollow station. It was addressed to Lord
Trundle and marked "FRAGILE".
"I wonder what it can be?" said old Stripey, the Porter.
"I don't know," replied Mr. Twinkle, the Station Master.
"But I'd better telephone Lord Trundle to let him know
it's arrived."

When he heard the news, Lord Trundle was very excited and rushed down to the railway station in his car. "Ah, at last!" he cried, looking at the great big wooden crate. "I've been waiting for this to arrive for weeks."

The crate was much too big to go inside Lord Trundle's car, so old Stripey and Mr. Twinkle helped him to tie it on to the roof rack, then away went the car, bouncing and rattling down the road.

The next day
Lord Trundle held
a meeting at Trundleberry Manor.
"As you all know," he began. "May Day isn't far away
now, and I wanted to do something really special in the
way of celebrations, so I've bought these!"
Lord Trundle pointed to the great big wooden crate.
"Musical instruments," he went on. "Fern Hollow is
going to have a brass band!"

Everyone had been given a musical instrument and the band had begun to practise, when suddenly the door burst open and in walked Snitch and Snatch. No one had invited them because they were always causing trouble. The two sneaky weasles had been peeping through the keyhole and had decided that they wanted to join the band.

"Give me the big drum," said Snatch.

"I'll have the sousaphone," said Snitch.

"I'm afraid there are only two triangles left," said Lord Trundle politely.

"We don't want your silly triangles!" screamed Snitch.

"And what's more, if we can't have the drum and sousaphone, then you won't have them for long either!"

And off they went, slamming the door behind them.

That night, Snitch and Snatch broke into Trundleberry Manor intending to steal the drum and sousaphone. But as Snitch was carrying the drum down the steps in front of the Manor, it slipped out of his hands.
BOOM BOOM BOOM
it went as it bounced down the steps.

The noise woke Lord Trundle, who jumped out of bed and looked out of his window, just in time to see the two weasles running away with the musical instruments. Quickly Lord Trundle telephoned Fern Hollow Police Station.

Constable Hoppit arrived a few minutes later, looking slightly out of breath from pedalling his bicycle so fast. "Don't worry, Lord Trundle," he panted. "We'll soon track the villains down. Which way did they go?"

Lord Trundle pointed
out the direction which
Snitch and Snatch had taken,
and followed P.C. Hoppit as the
Policeman raced off in pursuit.

"There they are," cried P.C. Hoppit. "Down on the river bank. We've got them now—they'll never be able to swim all the way across the Ferny with the drum and sousaphone!"

But the wily weasles had a plan. They
pushed the big drum out into the river
and jumped on top. Then Snitch began
to paddle with a stick, while Snatch held
onto the sousaphone.

Soon the weasles were halfway across
the river leaving Lord Trundle and P.C.
Hoppit standing helplessly on the bank.

It looked very much like Snitch and Snatch were going to get away, but suddenly the drum became caught in a strong current, and was swept away down river.

The terrified weasles clung onto the drum for all they were worth, but it was no use, because they were quickly swept over the waterfalls. Luckily for them, Mr. Whirlygill, the Ferryman, was watching and was able to drag them both out.

As a punishment P.C. Hoppit locked
Snitch and Snatch up in Fern Hollow
Police Station for a few days where they
missed all the May Day fun.
Lord Trundle's brass band was, of course,
a great success. They paraded around the
streets of Fern Hollow all afternoon,
before at last they stopped for a well-
deserved rest at the Jolly Vole,
where Mr. Crackleberry supplied
everyone with orange juice
and sandwiches!

MR. RUSTY'S NEW HOUSE

One morning Rufus Rusty woke up
with something dripping on his forehead.
PLIP PLIP PLIP.
"Oh no!" cried Rufus to his brother
Redvers who was in the lower bunk.
"The roof is leaking."
"Never mind," giggled Redvers.
"I'm quite dry down here!"

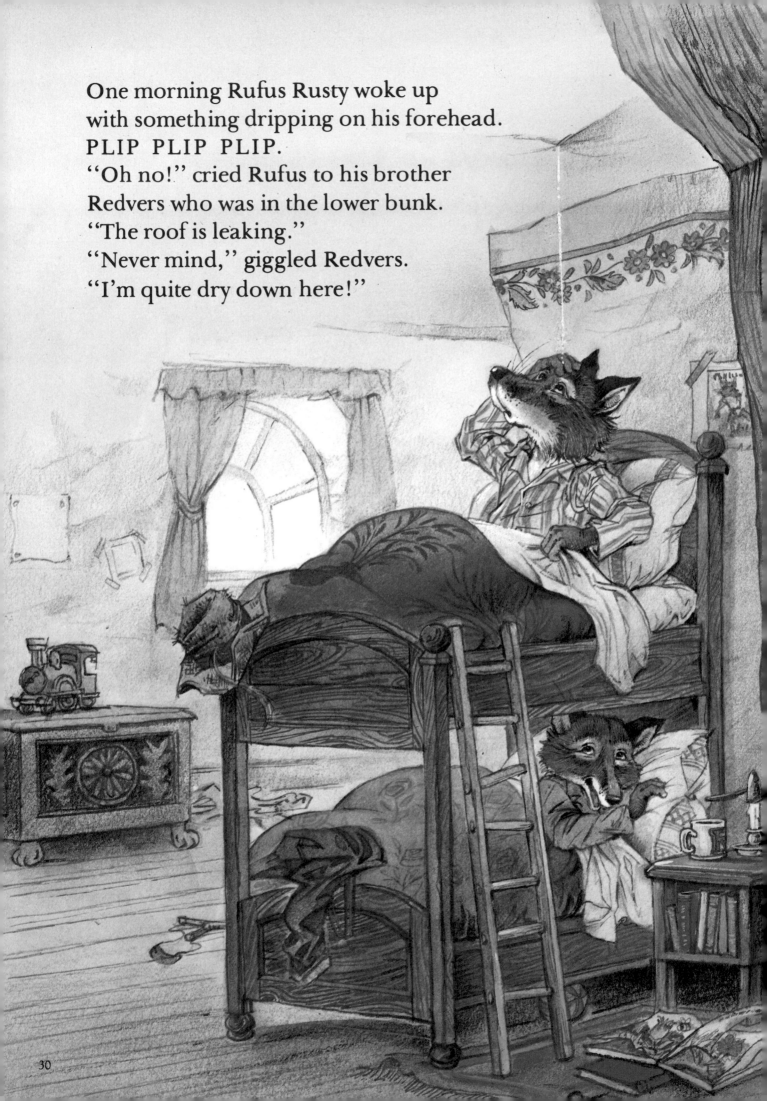

Rufus leapt out of his soggy bed and ran to tell his mother and father, but they were already running around with pots and pans trying to catch the rain, which was leaking into their bedroom. It was the same in Dusty's room.

"It's hardly worth having a roof at all if it's going to leak like this!" said Mrs. Rusty.

Eventually Mr. Rusty managed to find enough pots and pans to catch all the drips. Then, after eating his breakfast, he set off for work at the railway station, where he was the engine driver. As he left, Mr. Rusty closed the front door behind him—and it fell off!

All day long things went wrong with Mr. Rusty's house;
soot fell down the chimney, the windows stuck and
wouldn't open and Mrs. Rusty fell
through the floorboards which
had become rotten.
"Oh, I wish we had a new
house," she moaned.

That night there was a terrible thunder storm.
Lightening flashed around the sky and it rained cats and
dogs.

In the morning the River Ferny, which had become swollen with all the rain, overflowed and rushed down into the hollow where Mr. Rusty's house stood. The water crept up higher and higher until, at last, Mr. Rusty and his family had to climb up onto the roof.

When Mr. Periwinkle the Postman came riding down the lane and saw Mr. Rusty and his family all perched on their cottage roof, he was so surprised that he fell off his bicycle.

"Don't worry, Mr. Rusty," cried Mr. Periwinkle, scrambling to his feet. "I'll ride over to the fire station and get Alphonso Duff and Mr. Bouncer—they'll know what to do."

The Fern Hollow firemen soon arrived
and began the rescue operation,
extending the ladder on top of the fire
engine all the way across the floodwater
to the Rusty family's roof.

37

Rufus and Redvers thought
it was all great fun, until
they both lost their balance
as they were climbing along
the ladder and fell
in the water!

38

Mr. Prickles had been watching the rescue and, realising that the Rusty family would now have nowhere to live, he invited them to stay with him for a while. The kind hedgehog soon made a nice warm fire and Mrs. Prickles gave each of the Foxes a bowl of steaming hot soup.

Later in the day Mr. Rusty heard a lot of
noise outside Mr. Prickles's house and
went outside to see what was happening.
A little further down the lane Brock
Gruffy and a few other animals had
started to build Mr. Rusty a new house.

Mr. Rusty set to work himself at once.
There was plenty to be done; hammering
and sawing, cement to make and bricks to
lay. It was a lucky thing for Mr. Rusty and
his family that they had so many good
friends to help them.

It took quite a long time to build the house, but each day a little more was done. The walls grew up and the roof was put on.

The tiles were laid and
the windows and doors
were fitted, and at last
Mr. Rusty's new house
was finished.

Of course, all the furniture from the flooded house was useless, but Mrs. Rusty's friends each gave her bits and pieces from their own homes, and Mr. Chips the woodman arrived with lots of tables, chairs and cupboards which he had made.

44

That night Mr. Rusty held a house-warming party to thank all his friends for their kind help. It was a very jolly party. The air around Mr. Rusty's new house was filled with the sound of singing and laughter and the lights of the windows twinkled merrily in the darkness.

SPORTS DAY

It was still very early in the morning, but some of the Fern Hollow animals were already busily preparing for the Sports Day, which, as usual, was to be held in one of Farmer Bramble's fields. Spike and Patch had been given the job of painting the white lines for the running lanes.

Meanwhile,
on the edge of the
field, Mr. Chips whistled happily
to himself as he went about the business of
putting up a refreshments stand.
"It's beginning to look quite splendid, Mr. Chips."
exclaimed Mr. Acorn, who was supplying the cakes and
buns.
"It certainly is," agreed Mr. Crackleberry, rolling a big
barrel of orange juice off the back of his wagon.
"I hope the weather stays fine though—there's a big
black cloud over there on the horizon."

At Trundleberry Manor, Lord Trundle packed the sports day prizes into a trunk and carried them out to his car. He too noticed the dark cloud on the horizon, but he was in too much of a hurry to give it much thought and, jumping into the car, he drove off to the sports field.

Suddenly, as he was driving over the bridge by the Jolly Vole Hotel, Lord Trundle's car hit a big stone lying in the road.

It was such a hard bump
that the trunk containing
the prizes shot off the roof
rack and with a great
SPLOSH!
landed in the River Ferny.

Luckily the trunk floated, but it was soon caught in the current and swept away down the river. "Oh no!" panted Lord Trundle, rushing along the river bank. "What ever shall we do?"

The Sports Day prizes would
certainly have been lost if it had not
been for Sigmund Swamp, who was
out fishing, and seeing the trunk
floating by, cast out his line and
caught it, just as if it had been a
great big fish!

It turned out that Sigmund had quite forgotten that it was the Sports Day, and was very pleased when Lord Trundle offered him a lift in his car. By the time they arrived at the sports field, the tug of war was about to begin, but the big black cloud was now directly overhead.

Each of the two teams led by P.C. Hoppit and Brock Gruffy got a firm grip on the rope. Boris Blink slowly raised the starting pistol and — BANG — the contest began.

A few moments later the big black cloud burst.
The rain came pouring down and, in next to no
time, the field became waterlogged.
The tug of war teams slipped and slid around
in the mud, fell into the puddles and looked
quite ridiculous.

Everyone ran for the shelter of the trees or the refreshments stand,
where they all stood around looking very glum.
It looked as if the Sports Day would have to be cancelled.
The sky was now completely covered
with clouds and the rain was falling harder all the time!
Then Lord Trundle had a wonderful idea.
''Everyone is invited to Trundleberry Manor,'' he cried.
''We'll hold the Sports Day indoors!''
All the animals agreed that it was a fine idea and they
quickly made their way to the Manor.

The sack race was held in
the great hall, and was won by
Dipper Croaker, who, being
a frog, could hop further
and faster than anyone,
even in a sack!

The egg and spoon race up and down the main staircase was great fun. Clarence Hoppit was in the lead for most of the way, but he dropped his egg and Dusty Rusty won by a whisker.

Then came the special event, the bannister slide. The contestants slid down the bannister, flew off the end, and landed on a mattress. Spike Willowbank won this quite easily, but he overshot the mattress and landed on top of Brock Gruffy!

When the games were all over, Sigmund Swamp set up
his camera to take a picture of the prize giving ceremony.
"Smile everyone." said Sigmund.

Fern Hollow

MR. CHIPS'S HOUSE

MR. WILLOWBANK'S
COBBLER'S SHOP

MR. CROAKER'S WATERMILL

STRIPEY'S HOUSE

SCHOOL

THE JOLLY VOLE
HOTEL

RIVER FERNY

MR. ACORN'S
BAKERY

MR. RUSTY'S HOUSE

MR. PRICKLES'S HOUSE

POST OFFICE

BORIS BLINKS'S
BOOKSHOP

MR. TWINKLE'S
HOUSE

MR. TUTTLEBEE'S
SHOP

MR. THIMBLE'S
TAILORS SHOP

WINDYWOOD